rhcbooks.com

ISBN 978-0-7364-4298-5 (trade) — ISBN 978-0-7364-4299-2 (ebook)

Printed in the United States of America

10 9 8 7 6 5 4 3 2 1

THE GRAPHIC NOVEL

Random House 🏠 New York

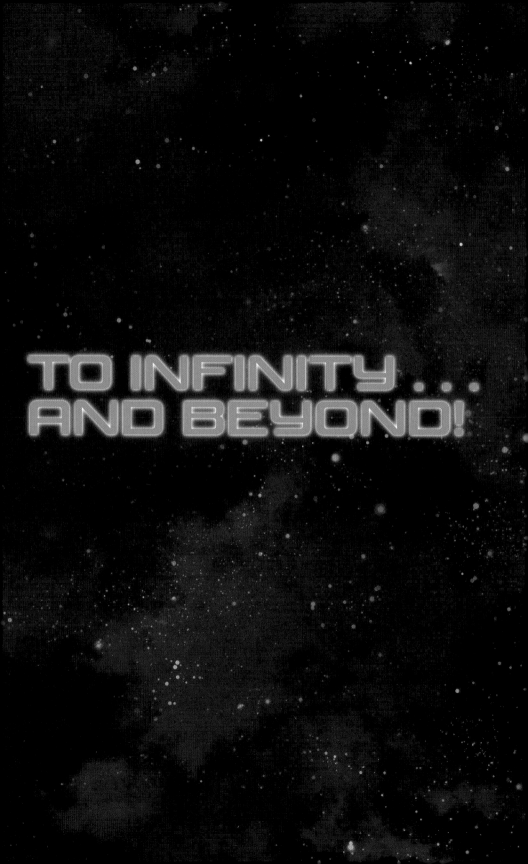

BUZZ
LIGHTYEAR

A skilled pilot and an experienced Space Ranger, *CAPTAIN BUZZ LIGHTYEAR* embraces every mission with heroic determination. While surveying the planet T'Kani Prime for possible life-forms, Buzz and Commander Alisha Hawthorne become stranded, along with their crew. Feeling responsible for their situation, and desperate to get everyone home safely, Buzz comes up against the planet's many dangers, an army of space robots, and even time itself! Can Buzz save everyone . . . or will his sense of self-reliance be his undoing?

STAR COMMAND

ALISHA HAWTHORNE

Simply put, *COMMANDER ALISHA HAWTHORNE* is an incredible Space Ranger. Everyone looks up to her, especially her best friend, Captain Buzz Lightyear. Buzz wishes he could be every bit as good as Alisha. When they become stranded on T'Kani Prime, Alisha heads the project that will help repair their spacecraft to take them home. As Buzz makes test flight after test flight, trying to save everyone, Alisha becomes his guiding light.

SOX

A robot companion in the form of an extraordinarily cute cat, *SOX* is Alisha's gift to Buzz after one of his missions. Sox's main job is to make Buzz happy. And while Sox might not always agree with Buzz's impulsive decisions, he's always willing to give the Space Ranger a helping paw in the form of lots of tech gizmos. Extremely intelligent and very resourceful, Sox becomes Buzz's sidekick . . . and unexpected friend.

STAR COMMAND

COMMANDER BURNSIDE

Having grown up on T'Kani Prime, *COMMANDER BURNSIDE* is not concerned with trying to get everyone back home. So when he becomes the new commander, Burnside decides they should focus on a new mission: constructing a laser shield capable of protecting everyone at the Star Command base from the planet's many dangers.

IZZY
HAWTHORNE

The young leader of the Junior Zap Patrol—a rough-around-the-edges group of cadets in training—*IZZY HAWTHORNE* is eager to prove herself. She wants to become one of the protectors of the new society springing up on T'Kani Prime. But her true dream is to be a Space Ranger, just like her grandmother Alisha. There's just one slight problem: Izzy is afraid of space!

THE JUNIOR ZAP PATROL

MAURICE
"MO" MORRISON

One of Izzy's fellow Junior Zap Patrol members, *MO* is a little lacking in direction. He hopes to find his place with the Junior Zap Patrol, but he doesn't like conflict and he really doesn't like taking risks. Mo would rather watch from the sidelines than take direct action. But when the Patrol joins up with Buzz, Mo must make a choice—sit back or step up and help save his team.

DARBY
STEEL

Unlike Mo, *DARBY* is a reluctant member of the Junior Zap Patrol. She's there only because of a court order—it seems that Darby spent a little time in prison! Darby does nothing by the book and has a passion for explosives. Though she may seem gruff, Darby is a perfect addition to Izzy's crew.

FEARSOME FOES

ZURG

A menacing force that descends upon the unsuspecting world of T'Kani Prime, the towering *ZURG* commands a seemingly unstoppable army of robots. Zurg appears obsessed with one thing only—capturing Buzz Lightyear. But why? And what is Zurg's ultimate goal? Will Buzz and the Junior Zap Patrol be able to stop this powerful foe before it's too late?

ZYCLOPES

The **ZYCLOPES** are the loyal robots that exist to serve Zurg and carry out his every whim. On T'Kani Prime, these automatons are tasked with one mission: locate Buzz Lightyear and bring him aboard Zurg's ship. They won't let anything or anyone stand in the way of obeying their orders.

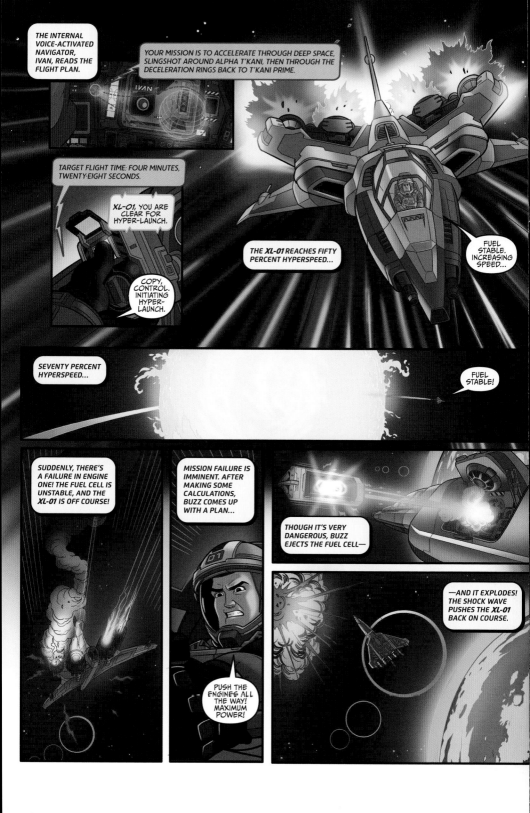

UH, CAPTAIN LIGHTYEAR? DO YOU NEED MY HELP?

NO, I CAN DO IT!

BUZZ?

ARE YOU *SURE*?

I CAN DO IT!

SENSORS INDICATE YOU HAD A NIGHTMARE. WOULD YOU LIKE TO TALK ABOUT IT?

NEGATIVE.

OKAY. BUT REMEMBER, MY MISSION IS TO *HELP* YOU. AND I'M *NOT* GIVING UP ON MY MISSION.

YEAH. YOU KNOW WHAT, SOX? I'M NOT GIVING UP ON *MY* MISSION, EITHER!

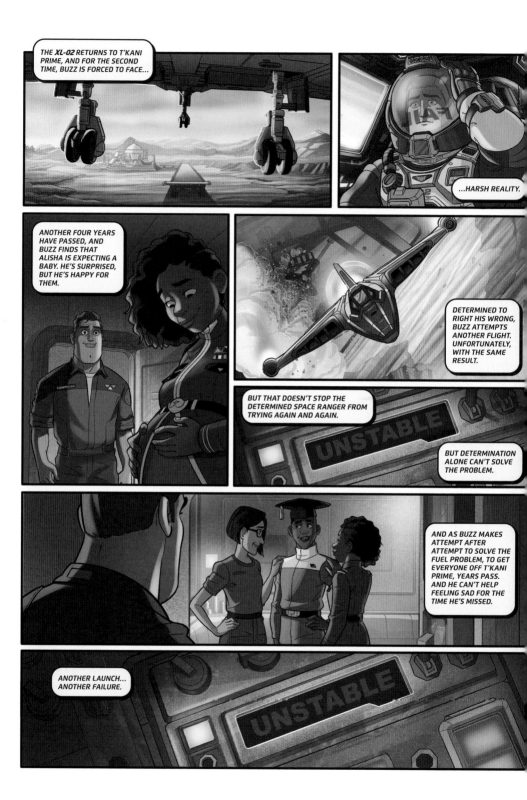

THE *XL-02* RETURNS TO T'KANI PRIME, AND FOR THE SECOND TIME, BUZZ IS FORCED TO FACE...

...HARSH REALITY.

ANOTHER FOUR YEARS HAVE PASSED, AND BUZZ FINDS THAT ALISHA IS EXPECTING A BABY. HE'S SURPRISED, BUT HE'S HAPPY FOR THEM.

DETERMINED TO RIGHT HIS WRONG, BUZZ ATTEMPTS ANOTHER FLIGHT. UNFORTUNATELY, WITH THE SAME RESULT.

BUT THAT DOESN'T STOP THE DETERMINED SPACE RANGER FROM TRYING AGAIN AND AGAIN.

BUT DETERMINATION ALONE CAN'T SOLVE THE PROBLEM.

UNSTABLE

AND AS BUZZ MAKES ATTEMPT AFTER ATTEMPT TO SOLVE THE FUEL PROBLEM, TO GET EVERYONE OFF T'KANI PRIME, YEARS PASS. AND HE CAN'T HELP FEELING SAD FOR THE TIME HE'S MISSED.

ANOTHER LAUNCH... ANOTHER FAILURE.

UNSTABLE

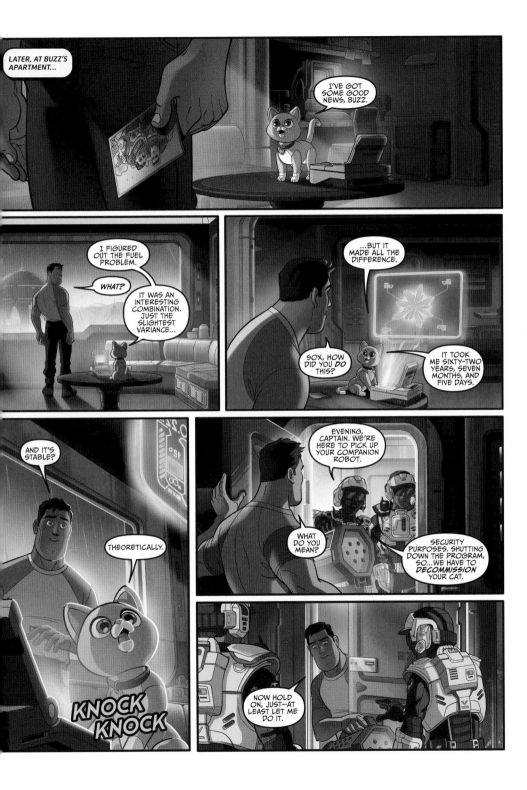

MOMENTS LATER...

CRASH

WHAM

AND WHEN THE GUARDS BURST IN, THEY FIND NO SIGN OF BUZZ OR SOX... THEY'RE ALREADY GONE.

BUZZ, WHERE ARE WE GOING?

WE'RE GOING TO SPACE!

WHAT?!

BUZZ HEADS FOR THE LAUNCHPAD, DETERMINED TO FINALLY FINISH HIS MISSION...

HEY! YOU'RE NOT AUTHORIZED TO BE IN THIS AREA!

FWIP

I DIDN'T KNOW YOU COULD DO THAT.

I BOUGHT YOU FIVE MINUTES.

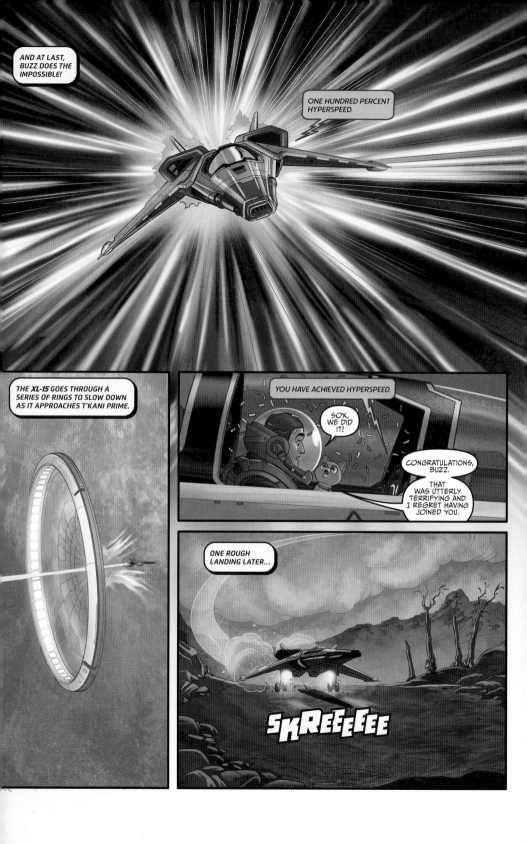

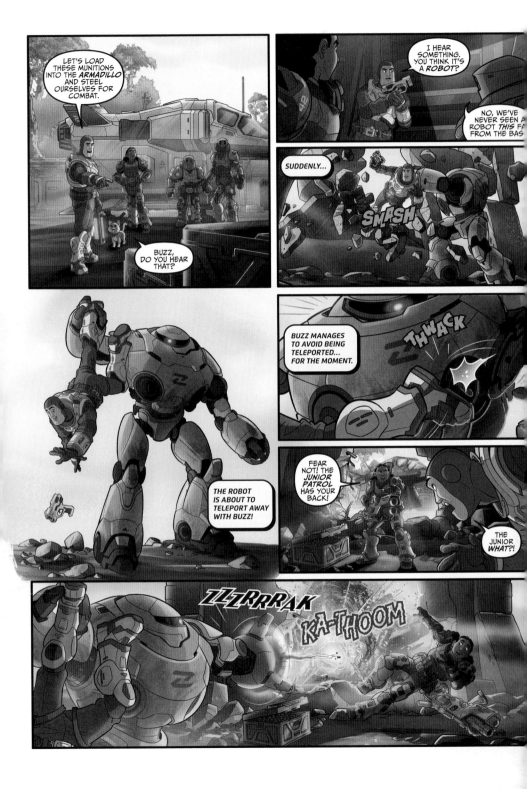

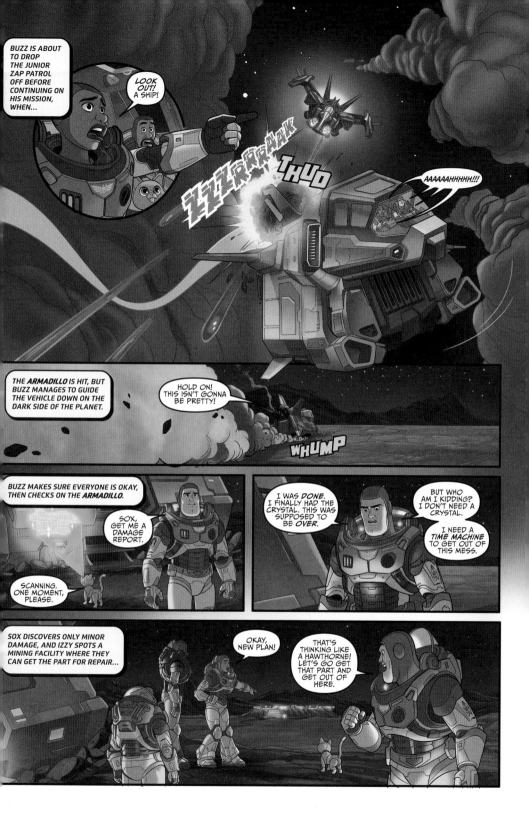

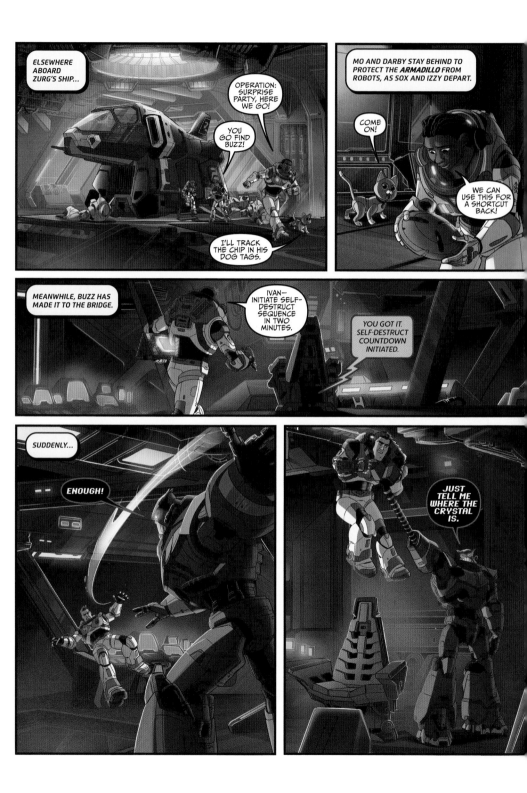

...INSERTS THE FUEL CRYSTAL...

THE OTHERS ARE ABOARD THE **ARMADILLO**, BUT BUZZ IS ADRIFT IN SPACE! HE QUICKLY GRABS ON TO THE **XL-15**...

...AND HEADS FOR THE **ARMADILLO**! BUT...THERE IS ONE SMALL PROBLEM...

...ZURG HAS RETURNED!

GOING SOMEWHERE?

YOU COULD HAVE USED THIS CRYSTAL TO MATTER AGAIN.

INSTEAD, IT WILL BE LIKE YOU WERE NEVER HERE.

SO... PREPARE TO DIE.

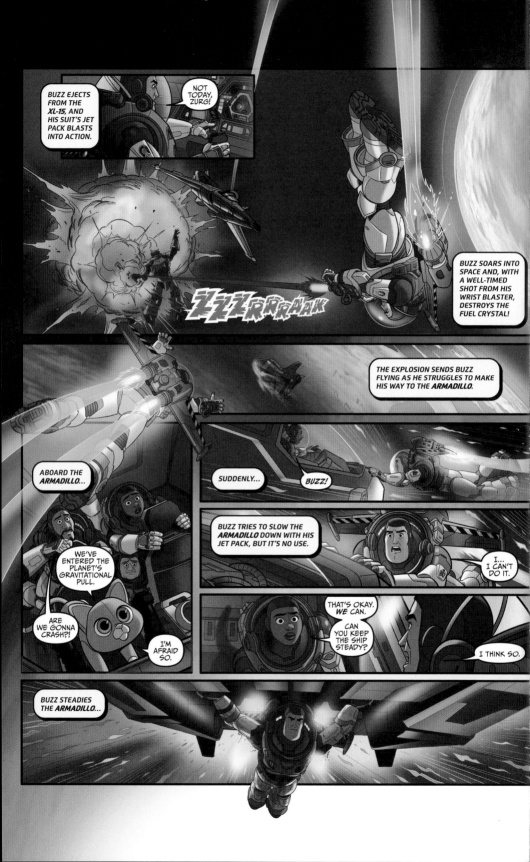

"To infinity . . ."

—COMMANDER
ALISHA HAWTHORNE
AND CAPTAIN
BUZZ LIGHTYEAR

"Congratulations, Buzz. That was utterly terrifying and I regret having joined you."

—SOX